TIME OF DRUMS

BOOKS BY JOHN EHLE

FICTION
Time of Drums
The Road
The Land Breakers
Lion on the Hearth
Kingstree Island
Move Over, Mountain

NONFICTION
The Free Men
Shepherd of the Streets
The Survivor

TIME OF DRUMS

A NOVEL BY
JOHN EHLE

HARPER & ROW, PUBLISHERS

New York and Evanston

As the bird by wandering,
as the swallow by flying,
so the curse causeless
shall not come.

Proverbs, 26:2

If you are a lady,
As I take you to be,
You won't crack a smile
When I tickle your knee.

*From North Carolina
folklore*

TO ROSIE

CHAPTER ONE

I would like first to tell you about the place I lived when my brother arrived to join me, this being in Virginia, but I would present myself in poor light if I did not first mention to you that my life up to that point had been affected by two matters: the death of my wife, after we had been married but a short time, and my alienation from my family, particularly my father. My wife was named Anna Morla. She was the third daughter of a poor farmer and I was the third son of a wealthy one, and our families lived near each other in a mountain valley with a little river running through it, one deep enough for swimming, an idyllic place, and that river was our courting road, our site of poetry and dreaming, both of us imagining a family, each of us for two years of courtship sneaking out of the house chipped and broken plates and cups, torn and tattered sheets—anything with which we might start our own housekeeping. And when finally we ran off and married, my father on our return, after much lecturing in his anger, did let me have sixty rocky acres of land for my own, and did come together with others of that mountain community to build us a small house, and did lend me a plow and a hoe and an ax and a cow and an ox, so in April we took our broken things to our own land and built our first fire in our own place together.

A year or so later, largely because of the work we had to do to survive, she died, and I buried her in the land and rocks which had killed her, so in a sense I had killed her, and my father had seen to it. In desperation I went to him and demanded a loan of money so I could go off some place where every tree and rock did not remind me of her. He said no, no, that I had made my bed and must lie in it, so on the next night I left that place, and I wandered from one town to another in the South, seeking work, finding none, seeking companionship, finding it often but moving on, seeking some woman to fill my heart again, becoming more harsh in my manner, burying deeper the whispers of tenderness and gentleness which once I had known in abundance, until when the war began I was ready for a war. This was the war between the North and the South, and I as a Southerner so distinguished myself in the first battle, the one on the Bull Run River near Manassas Junction, that I was elected an officer by my fellow soldiers on that very ground. As an officer I had at last a way to advance, and even though advancement sometimes required the risking of my life, I risked it willingly. After two years of war, after seven battles and many skirmishes, I was a colonel in command of my regiment of mountain soldiers.

In December, 1862, in Northern Virginia, the vast enemy army was wintered down across the river from us. My youngest brother arrived, a recruit to my own outfit. He came to the log barn I had chosen for my headquarters and the gathering place for my men; we had made a fireplace out of stone, mud and sticks, and it burned brightly day and night, and petitioners sat on boxes and benches along the walls waiting for me or my aide to hear them—soldiers hoping for a furlough, wives looking for their men, parents wanting to know where their boy was, people sick and well, awake and asleep, belching, complaining, insolent, indolent, many of them tired to death of this war yet unwilling to let go of it, none of us knowing how to let go of it and I not really wanting to, for I had nothing else then.

I recall that at the moment my brother arrived I was listening to the rambling, baffling excuses of a soldier found drunk on duty, a soldier I liked because he did have a sense of humor in spite of his life failures. My aide, Sergeant Silver, interrupted to tell me that the new volunteers had arrived, our December shipment of human beings, about thirty of them, farmers and planters and storekeepers, young and old, and he said my youngest brother was among them. At once I felt a jolt of apprehension, for I was ill prepared to expose myself to reminders of family or home, and I was much too busy here in the shadow of a new campaign to bend to filial needs.

My brother appeared at the doorway across the room, a boy only sixteen or seventeen years old. He was as tall and slender as I had been at his age. He had a big blond mop of hair and the blue eyes of my family, the firm chin and large mouth of my mother, and about him was a blatant trustfulness which I suspected would stand him in poor stead here, particularly since he would be conspicuously the colonel's brother. I pretended I didn't recognize him and retreated to the north corner, which was my private place to sit and hold counsel. I admit I was peculiarly confused by the appearance of a bit of flesh and blood which was related to me and had a right to intimacy with me who avoided intimacy, who was vulnerable no longer to anybody.

Sergeant Silver brought me a cup of coffee. "Your brother looks like you, sir," he said.

"I wonder if he's housebroken," I said.

Silver laughed. "The other recruits take well to him."

"Their mascot is he?"

"He might not be a problem to you, sir."

"He was twelve or thirteen when I left home, and I think of him that way. Send him off, can you?"

"Oh, I don't think so, sir. He's one of ours now."

He stood by the doorway to the porch, smiling at me, dressed in homespun civilian clothes, his best I suspect, watching me intently, frankly studying me, no doubt to see if I looked like papa or mama or Jesse or Phillip. I roused myself reluctantly and approached him, stopped close to him. I could even touch the doorway which framed him. I was no doubt frowning at him, but he had my father's smile, which was my smile, on his shiny-skinned, trusting face, my face, his teeth glistening with my family's spit, my mother's blue eyes blinking at my eyes looking at me, my brother's tongue coming out of my mother's mouth, my father's blond hair unruly over my brother's forehead, and about him was my father's smell of farmwork and of fields and sweat. "What you here for, Woofer?" I asked.

"Is that you, Owen?" he said, that damn smile broadening into a squirrellike grin.

Few men here called me Owen. I was the Colonel. The Colonel says we drill today, the Colonel says not to leave firewood on the road, the Colonel will give you hell if he finds that there woman in here, the Colonel said we won't move out till tomorrow, the Colonel said to wait for the doctor, soldier ...

"How's everybody at home, Woofer?"

"Mama's not b-b-been sick a day, she claims, but she don't b-b-bend over so easy now, Owen. I mean, when she b-bends over at the fireplace, she's a long time straightening, and I notice she sends Nell to do the milking for she can't squat and get up without holding to a fence rail."

"That so?"

"Papa's not more'n a hairsbreath b-better when it comes to rainy weather. He gets to hurting in his joints like a fire's about to flare up, but he won't set, even so, he has to work his day through, though sometimes I see the sweat standing on his face like it was splattered there, and his eyes are more slits than ever, as if he's gr-grinding himself to stand it. A heart attack come on him a year ago, you know."

"Uh-huh," I said. "I didn't know."

"You look so much like papa it's scary," he said.

"We can forget the family for now," I said. I noticed a few soldiers listening to us and I felt exposed and vulnerable.

"But you're bigger'n he is, and better looking. Nell told me I'd probably never see anybody more like a commander of soldiers than you."

Somebody laughed and several men got to snickering and

4

winking at each other. I stepped out into the road to get away from them; I was embarrassed, of course, but I admit also I was pleased to be complimented—I am more vain than I ought to be. Also I was warmed suddenly to be reminded of Nell, my sister, who had been about twenty when I left home. I had helped rear her, as older brothers have a liking to do sometimes. I had often comforted her on occasions, when she had lost a boyfriend, or when nobody had seemed to notice her at church or a dance, or when she was gloomily predicting she would not grow up to be pretty—and she wasn't pretty, to be honest about it, that was fate's one miserable trick on Nell, but she was generous and kind and a lovely person, and I loved her. How long ago, how long ago, another lifetime.

The road was sloppy from the afternoon rain and was fuming with odors of horses and mules and excrement and food and garbage; even the puddles of rainwater were putrid. "Listen, I don't care to hear any more about the family, Woofer," I said.

"Why n-n-not, Owen?" he said, the big smile on his face, trusting and utterly open and friendly.

"A man learns to live within himself as he grows older. You'll see."

"Is that what p-p-papa d-did?"

"What you stuttering for? You still stutter?"

"Only when I'm nervous. I st-stutter once in a great while. Papa says I do it when I want to."

"I can't tell you how far away the family is to me here. It's another life entirely, and it gets complicated to try and live two lives at once. A soldier gets so he doesn't care, anyway."

"I been waiting to get to be eighteen so's I could join—"

"As a brother I advise you to go on home. We don't need boys here."

He was smiling at me even yet, but more wonderingly, somewhat questioningly, which was disconcerting in itself. "I'd like to stay, Owen."

"Well, I don't know why you would want to. The war will be

5

over by the end of next spring, before you're trained worth a damn. You'll not get to be much of a soldier by then."

"Owen—"

"I've got no time to diaper-tend you, Woofer."

"You won't n-need to worry about me, Owen."

"God damn, now even the family starts coming in on me."

"I thought a soldier got so he didn't care," he said. There he stood, staring back at me, firm and steady, clear-eyed, smiling. "I thought you didn't care about anything, you got so toughened by it."

Jesus, what nerve. I touched his face, laid my palm alongside his cheek. "You tell them I said hello," I said, and pushed him backward a step or two. But he showed no fear, no sign of obeying either. "Mama know where you are?" I asked.

"I'll write her."

"You'll hurt her, too. She always favored you."

He was flushed in his face now, but was not angry or critical. "Owen, I'm staying," he said.

"Don't aggravate me, boy. I'm used to having my way around here, even if I didn't have it at home."

"I'd find another unit, that's all, so the only thing you'd gain is saving yourself some trouble. It is you that you're worried about, ain't it, Owen?"

"What sort of damn question is that?"

"Yes, it is yourself you're concerned about, not me."

I turned from him, walked away, but he followed me, sloshing, slipping in the mud. I stopped at a place where I could see the camp spread out before us on the hillside, several thousand tents and shelter halves and crudely made huts thrown together of logs and rocks and canvas and blankets and fence rails and saplings and mud and string, many of them with squat stone-and-mud chimneys glowing hot as women's mouths, and the camp was making sharp noises and burps and sighs, belches, a bell way off, a piece of metal being struck, a man shouting "No, you son of a bitch," a cavalry horse nickering, an artillery mule

6

braying, the distant notes of a bugle, the crackles of fires, the squish of wheels turning through mud, a dog barking, horses' hoofs plodding, tin cups striking against wooden water buckets, water sloshing close by when a soldier cursing threw slop onto the road, a train approaching, its bell tolling, bringing more recruits sitting on top of boxcars ogling the sights of the horde, this conglomerate, oozing blanket of men and animals and huts and tents covering the earth, steaming with its own heat, speaking like the water-driven gears in a mill, rasping softly its own geared sounds, humming to itself, warming itself with a thousand fires, each burst and flash of fire dying within its own body, inside the circle of itself, choked on light, strangled by itself just as the camp would strangle any man not sure of himself and would someday surely strangle itself.

"It's enough to scare a man, Owen, I admit," Woofer said.

Owen, Owen, Owen.

"It smells keen, don't it, Owen? The recruiters don't mention the stink of the war."

"War has a smell with gunpowder and sulphur in it. This is only winter camp."

"I'm not complaining. I wouldn't want to come into a new place and start fussing about the way it is."

"Why not?"

"I mean, I'm not the one in charge."

"I'll say you're not. Nobody's even listening to you."

"I try to look on the b-b-bright side, Owen."

"Stop your damn grinning like papa."

"I can't help it, Owen, you looking so serious and deathlike."

He kept grinning at me, so I had to smile. He was only a boy, a buck private soldier facing down a colonel like that.

"You got your nerve, buddy," I told him.

"Papa always said I was a nervy one."

"You got nerve enough for them?" I asked, and pointed out across the river where a glow was lighting the skies, as if dawn was breaking over that way.

7

"What is it you mean, Owen?" he said. "Another camp over there?"

"The Yanks," I said, and we stood in the hush that always followed the uttering of that word. "You can hear them singing sometimes. You can hear their guns sometimes, practicing. They've been over there since we beat them at Fredericksburg. You got nerve enough to fight them?"

He stood there smiling at me, but the smile had got lame and twisted, and he coughed suddenly. "I didn't come for the war so much as for finding you."

"They could come across that river tonight."

"In this cold weather?"

"Or we might go across it. Jackson has no set way of fighting."

He rubbed his face with the palms of his hands, warming his skin. "I need to talk to you, Owen, soon as we can get warm," he said, "about a woman-need I've got."

"You'll want to attend to your own needs," I said. I saw that the other recruits were still standing outside my headquarters, next to a little stall that served as my bedroom. They were cold, even though they were well dressed, with thick homespun suits and with heavy boots and shoes on. Some of them wore hats. A soldier coming by said, "Colonel, you ready to welcome them?"

"Yes. Call the men," I said.

My men were hard fighters. They were not drill-field soldiers. They were rough in body and manners, and they were accustomed to winning. They had spent the year together in battles from Kernstown and Front Royal to Fredericksburg, which was only just over, its smoke still in their hair and clothes. Their skin was leather-weathered, as was mine, their hands were calloused in layers of hide, their eyes were as cold as water from a spring, their stomachs were corroded by putrid flesh and polluted water. We had seen friends fall in illness and in battle; we had seen them fail in courage too, become limp flesh broken at the thin bones of the heart, though more often I have known men worn down in body, their hands scarcely able to hold up the gun they

8

fired, who fought on. Physical strength was not the answer, but toughness was. Not brutality. I have no use for that, though some of my soldiers suffer from it. Brutal soldiers are about to collapse on the other side of the wall. Most of my men don't need hate in order to be committed. They don't even need a political cause in order to be committed. What they need is each other and this regiment, they need being part of it; we need each other. I need them, certainly. We all come from the mountains, all have the same hefty degree of dogged independence. The army had had a hell of a time putting up with us, but it owed us more than our pay.

They were sloshing up the road now to take part in the welcome. They appeared two or three or four from a hut or tent, dirty and grizzly as bears. "Give 'em hell, Colonel," they grumbled at me as we walked past. About two hundred of them assembled, pushing, shoving each other. They formed a circle around the recruits, who were damn wary by now, who were clean and well cared for by comparison.

"Oh, you sorry bastards," one of the older soldiers said.

"You'll see hell by spring."

"You bastards, why you come here clean?"

A soldier approached one of them, a young, shiny-faced kid. Carefully, deliberately he took off the recruit's overcoat and put it on his own scavengerlike body.

"Ain't you Mr. Marshall from home?" the boy said to him, choking on fear.

"You keep your mouth shut when you talk to me," the soldier said.

A soldier poked his finger into the face of a recruit, a man about thirty-five, a planter, I suppose, neatly dressed. "Come out of that there hat," the soldier said to him.

"I see his arms poking out, so he's in there," another soldier said. "No need for him to say he's not in there."

Captain Crawford, one of my officers, a refined man, too refined for initiation ceremonies, motioned for the recruit to take off his hat, a splendid felt one, but the man was too proud or scared to understand. So two or three soldiers roughly knocked it off him by upending him. "Now come out of them there boots," a soldier said to him.

"Get out of them wool pants," another said to him, even as he struggled with his boots.

"Out of that there wool shirt."

They stripped him. And so it went as the outer clothing of all the volunteers were taken from them, and they in turn were furnished with the ragged, lice-infested clothes my soldiers provided, and with shoes that had been broken open, and with torn hats and caps.

I saw Sergeant Willis approach a middle-aged man who was mustached, a farmer from Boone, I believe. "Take them mice out of your mouth," he said.

"Come out 'er that bunch of beard, soldier."

"This 'un has got too long a head hairs, Sergeant."

Off came the beards, mustaches, and long hair, knives whacking at them. When this new frenzy was over, lanterns were brought forward to reveal for inspection the thirty recruits, their hair hacked short, all of them deplorably dressed and shod.

A wagon was rolled forward and I mounted it and called for the men to stop their plundering and give me their attention, which came belatedly, with much grumbling. A mountain regiment tolerates discipline only as it chooses to. I said, "I'm up here to tell you new men, if you have any complaints or get to feeling lonely, to go see Captain Crawford here."

The veterans laughed, for they enjoyed an officer deriding another officer, especially Crawford, who was old-maidenish in his ways.

"If you feel a draft, he's the one to go to," I said. "Now then, if any of you plays the bagpipe, I wish you'd tell me. Anybody play the pipes?"

The recruits shook their heads.

"I wish somebody did. We had a bagpipe player but he got

10

shot six times at Fredericksburg, which shows what you can expect of the Yanks, for he had his pipes on, he was playing. We sometimes go into battle with pipes playing. Anybody play the guitar or fiddle?"

Three men held up their hands.

"Sergeant Silver, give those three men a hut near me. I hope you'll play every night or so, for I want to hear it. Anybody play the drums?"

Nobody raised his hand.

"Well, we can't have it all, boys," I said. "We have a bugle player but don't use him, for I don't like the bugle. We get up in the morning by the bugle calls from nearby regiments. When you hear their bugles, drag yourself out of bed and stand out in the road to be counted. And when the bugles blow for drill, we go down the hill to the brigade's drill field and drill for a while, though not as long as the other two regiments do. Mountain troops can shoot better than the others can, can track an enemy through a woods, can live on herbs and nuts, can heal their own wounds—I contend we are the best fighters and the poorest soldiers in the world."

My veteran soldiers, a few of them, yelled out agreement.

"But we will drill a little while every day and try to look like soldiers anyway. I don't expect you to look as favorable as the sassy-assed Virginians or the big-balled South Carolinians, who come here for a pleasant winter and like to walk arm in arm."

My men liked jokes like that, about the lordly ones around us.

"The South Carolinians started this war two years ago so they could have an excuse to leave home, for they were bored with their riches and shiftlessness, and Virginia is the sorry place it's to be fought in, and in between these two mountains of conceit is our valley of North Carolina, and we're in the thick of it, thanks to them, and will have to win it for them, for surely Virginia and South Carolina can't win it for themselves."

A mighty shout went up from the soldiers, and much laughter. Off to one side a fist fight broke out with the suddenness

11

of a summer storm, and as quickly subsided.

"Now I've been here for about two years, and I want you to help me in our next spring's campaign, that's all I ask of you, or of myself. I want you to stay with me wherever Jackson sends us till then, and if that takes us into the Yank guns, you come along. We want to end this war properly. I want you to know that the standard of this regiment has never gone down. My men have never bent, even at the gates of Richmond, even at Sharpsburg. Dirty we may be, shot through and torn we have been, but we will march thirty miles of a night if Jackson tells us to, and go the next day till he says to stop, and we'll be ready to fight Yanks before we rest or eat. You hear me?"

A murmur went through the mob of men. They were romantic in their souls about the regiment, as I well knew, as I was.

"Sleep on the ground, if needs be. Better that than lose our land. Eat nothing, if needs be. You won't die as long as you keep moving. If you get thirsty, spit and swallow it. Don't come nagging to me about any of it—where you're to sleep, what you're to eat or anything else like that, for I don't run my regiment that way. The Yankees are like that. In my regiment we go our way, every man making out for himself until the fighting starts. You sleep where you fall, you eat what you find—and tomorrow there'll be a food issue, a pound and a quarter of corn meal to each man and half a pound of fatback. That'll be for the day, and that's so most every day, except now and then we get a head of cabbage for the regiment."

The soldiers laughed, and there now was a nostalgic quality, a mellow friendliness to their laughter, for we were talking about our common woes, ones we had endured together so long they seemed like friends.

"Where the hell do the potatoes go, will you tell me?" I shouted. "Who is going off with the potatoes?"

"Amen, Colonel. Tell them, Colonel."

"Where are the onions?"

12

"Don't see 'em, Colonel."

"I tell you where they are," I whispered hoarsely, as if sharing a secret with them. "The Commissary Department takes them and sells them and makes themselves rich, and their mouths and their guts are full of gold."

A roar of approval, a harsh, reverberating shout shook the place. I could always win a big reaction to any criticism of the rations. I jumped down from the wagon and told Captain Crawford to dismiss the men—it did not occur to me that we might have trouble with them tonight. Brutality seeps into some soldiers, as I said earlier. I should have stayed out there with them, but I went into the building and began talking with an elderly soldier, a planter from near Burnsville, who wanted a furlough; I was trying to help him find an excuse to justify one when I heard shouting, a viciousness to it, and I moved as quickly as I could to the door. In my mind was a vision of some mischief happening to Woofer.

It was not Woofer, but another boy about his age; a group of the men had stripped him naked and had mounted him astride a porch pole and were declaring him to be a king of the Confederacy, or some such foolishness. The boy was screaming in pain and terror. "Christ a' mercy," I shouted, and moved into the mob, which had got out of Captain Crawford's control; he was white as a sheet and speechless with fear. "Put him down," I shouted.

But the men paid no attention to me; they were off on their own spree, and they started down the hill, the poor boy screaming, holding to the pole for dear life.

"Let him down, damn you," I said. Lieutenant McGregor, my one courageous officer, and I began to pull men away from the pack, but our efforts did no good, for the cluster of men was too tight and wild, even their eyes were battle-wild now, their teeth were showing. I don't mean all my men; only forty or fifty of them. They moved down the hill shouting and singing.

13

I struck a trembling porch pole with the flat of my hand and hurled it into the road. "Get back to your damn huts," I said to the others. "My God."

Woofer appeared before me and I stopped dead in my tracks looking into that mass of innocence and astonishment, for he was open-mouthed and woefully incredulous. "Law, Owen, law a' mercy," he said.

"Why, law a' mercy yourself," I said and pushed past him and moved inside, went to my own chair and sat there listening to the cries of that frightened kid until at last they quit and the customary, ordinary commotions of the camp were all that remained to be heard, they and the fire-crackling noises nearby. What the hell, I thought, God knows, God knows what gets into them. I went into my room and pulled off my boots and jacket and threw them aside. When Woofer came to my door and watched me, I said, "You got no business in here, boy."

He seemed to pay no attention to that at all. "Law a' mercy, Owen, they went wild out there," he said.

"Yeh," I said, lying down on my bed. I was smelly of sweat and uncomfortable, and my feet came out from under the covers; I was too long for the bed; I'm 6'2" and the bed had been made for somebody else, some short officer. Woofer pulled a blanket around my feet and tucked it in. "Don't be so damn helpful, you hear me?" I said. "You'll never be a soldier." I waved him back and pulled the blanket up under my chin, the wool scratchy and itchy on me.

"You want a hot pig, Owen?" he said, that being the term my mother had for hot bed bricks or a hot-water pan.

"No, I don't want anything. Stop reminding me, anyway. Get on, go on."

He left reluctantly, glancing back at my door even as he crossed the main room.

My stomach had turned sour. I ought to get up and take a Brandeth pill, I knew, but I won't throw up if I lie still, I told myself.

14

Sergeant Silver came in, a scrawny man, small and maybe fifty. He never shaved properly, and he would cut his hair once every week by holding it between his fingers and cropping it even with his knuckles. His face was warty. He revered me for some reason—I don't know why. He liked me and trusted me.

"Did they hurt that boy?" I asked.

"A few bruises, I suppose, and they scared him."

"Yeh. Did they beat up any of the others of them tonight?"

"One or two, once they got started."

"They come in new, come in with clean clothes and clean skin, no filth and lice on them, and the men want them to be lousy like they are."

"After next spring," he began, "we can go home, Colonel."

"One more campaign, that's all. I mean it, you hear? One more. I want to see it through whole, with my regiment whole. Is that too much to ask for a third year?"

"No, Colonel."

"God knows I never had a chance until this war to be anything except a plowman and a butcher of pigs in winter, a hunter of bears come fall. God knows. But I'll go back to being nobody rather than continue much longer in the war, Silver."

"Yes, sir. I know. We stretch ourselves thin."

"I've forgotten what affection is, Silver. It trembles inside me, shakes like a scared child. I realized that tonight. I don't know how to touch my brother. God knows, I've almost forgot myself entirely."

I never set myself the task of training Woofer. He seemed always to be nearby, watching me, that's all. So I began converting him into a soldier as best I could, while he continued to awaken old kindnesses in me. I would set him down by my nighttime fire and lecture him in the routine truths of my profession. "A soldier must be his own man first of all. I have had many professions—a smith's helper, a miller for a while in Virginia, a farmer in three places, a hunter. I was some of these as long or

15

longer than I've been a soldier, but none of them is as intense. A miller doesn't kill people or risk his life. When one endures two campaigns and has lost hundreds of his men, has killed men —are you listening?"

"I'm not going to be able to kill many people, I'm afraid, Owen," he said.

"A soldier—that's his profession."

He sniffed and thought about it. "I'm not going to be good at it, I'm afraid, Owen." He had picked up Silver's little dog and was stroking it; he had her on his lap. "Papa got him two long-eared hounds from England, named one Antony and the other Cleopatra." He was always talking about the people back home, and the family. He would find different ways to snag my interest in them. He told me about the Plovers, who usually bore blond girls, one a year, all of them neat of bone, growing up like pretty weeds. He told about the house I had left, a little place which he said locust trees and poplars were thicketing all about.

"I don't want to know about that," I told him. "I'm trying to live my own life free of that now."

But he would persist; he had a gentle way of doing as he pleased. He never argued, he simply persevered. He would take the long way around and bring up the same subject again, cloaking it differently, seeking a way to make it more acceptable to me. "We had this harvest party last fall at the house, Owen, as we've done ever year since time began, and none of the planters came."

"They always came when I was a boy."

"Yes, but no planter came to papa's house at all, it being common knowledge that he favors the North, and the farmers who came divided into two groups, those who favor the North and those that favor the South, and when Lena Andrews, whose husband is off fighting with the Southern army, got to dancing with a Yank sympathizer, her mother-in-law yanked her out of the circle, interrupted Plover and the others that were playing the music, and shouted at her, 'My boy's in the army, and I want

16

to know what you're doing out there twirling your butt with him?' "

"Papa laughed, I'll wager you," I said, laughing. "Didn't he?"

Woofer winked at me. "What you care about papa for, Owen?" he said.

With these daily inducements I began to think more kindly about the valley at home, to recall how pretty it was with every family having its own land and house on it, barn, sheds, smokehouse, springhouse, crib, with cows, chickens, sheep, steers, a horse or two. All proud people, craftsmen most of them, not like many lowland farmers with their single crop. I began to taste in my mouth the sweet and pungent foods and in my heart the sweet and bitter feelings of olden days. I wanted to go home again, that was the truth of it, though I didn't yet dare admit it. I suppose it was inevitable that Woofer would cause this change to begin in me.

As for him, he became my companion, the dirty smiling shadow of myself, even my conscience in a friendly way.

On Sunday morning Sergeant Silver would shave me, then I would put on a clean uniform, one of two that I owned, and my belt and holster—and I must say I looked like an officer. I was lean and fit; I could not get fat on Confederate rations. I left my hair rather long; most mountain men did, both up home and here—except, of course, for recruits. My hair is rather full anyway; it's blond, almost as blond even at my age as it was when I was Woofer's, and thick. My eyebrows are full too. I have blue eyes, really quite dark blue, extraordinarily dark.

As I say, I was rather pleased with my appearance on Sundays. I told myself I was quite a handsome fellow and did indeed look like a colonel, and did indeed look like a prospective general, which was a matter of particular concern to me just then. The general over me was aged and no longer able to command on the field.

About ten o'clock I would go with Captain Crawford, himself

rather drab and dumpy, a man my age, about thirty-three, with an emotion-laden, baby face; we would go on an inspection round of the regimental area, which was one long, eroded street running uphill and down. Our hundred or more hovels lined each side of the street. They were named Last Chance, Larry's Best, Lost Cove, the Womb, Welcome Home, Go Away ... At inspection the men sat in front of their respective huts, coming to attention only when Captain Crawford and I approached, usually in company with a lieutenant, and always with the sergeant of the respective company.

One hut had a new floor. I ordered the company's sergeant to have the saplings removed, and we found under them several jugs of whiskey, which I was pleased to confiscate. "This is a damaging stuff," I told the hut's five men, who were mournfully attentive. "You're quite fortunate to be rid of it. Come by at seven and I'll give you a taste of it."

Woofer had fallen into Company B, which was by army tradition the last one to be inspected. I went into his hut this next Sunday, the Sunday before Christmas, and found that it had three bunks, each made of saplings, each having one filthy wool blanket. The ceiling was canvas. There was a dirt floor. The walls were of saplings and mud, the fireplace was of rocks and mud, and beside it were three unwashed tin plates, an iron frying pan, an iron pot, all dirty, a water bucket without a handle, one piece of beef turned blue at the edges over which skippers were crawling.

I went outside and looked over the two hutmates. "Who owns the piece of beef?" I asked.

"I own it, sir," a soldier named Betsy Mallard said. He belched, no doubt from nervousness. "Sour stomach, sir." He was about forty-five, wiry and wry, wrinkled severely of face, a farmer and hunter, as I well knew. A veteran.

"How do you get skippers out of meat, Betsy?"

"I like skippers in my meat, sir."

18

"But if a new man doesn't, what would you tell him?"

"Yes, well, it can be done with a cup of hot coffee if he drops his meat into it, for the dear skippers will rise to the surface soon enough."

"Very well answered. Where are you from—from Newland?"

"Madison County, west from where you growed up, yourself, until you went away to make your fortune, sir."

"You've been in the army since the start, haven't you?"

"Aye, sir, by your side and at your heels, sir, and tired of it, begging your pardon, sir." He was squinting into the sun, unhappily reviewing his status as a soldier. "It bothers me to have a wife and a boy to home, and me be here, and if you could see your way clear to let a two-year man go visit for a short spell—"

"And not come back?"

"I'm not a deserter, sir. I'm not, like so many others are."

"Maybe, maybe." I moved on to the other hutmate, a tall, straggly, dour fellow with a hawk face, with thin lips which just now because of nervousness were drawn tight across his teeth. He wore black clothes, not army issue at all—he had not so much as an army shirt on, but he wore an army cap on his head. I believe once he had been brought to me for drunkenness. "Martin, is it?" I asked.

"Yes, sir. Martin Luther," he said.

"It wasn't Luther when I last talked with you a year ago."

"I've changed it," he said. "In a dream an angel said to change to a holy name."

"An angel? Here?"

"In a flash of fire, Colonel, in that hut there, crouched by the fireplace to warm hisself, last winter soon after I was saved."

"I never realized angels got cold."

"I—believe they must, Colonel."

"It wasn't the same angel that was sent to the Virgin Mary, was it?"

19

Martin blinked at me, astonished. "Why, I don't know."

"He didn't say anything to you about it, and made no proposition of any sort to you?"

He stared at me dismayed. "God will strike us down," he whispered hoarsely. He was trembling, was glancing about to see if the lightning bolts had begun falling.

"I've never liked the idea of angels lurking about army camps," I said. "If you see another one, you are to tell Captain Crawford here, and, Captain, you are to put the angel in the stocks until we can find out what his mission is."

"I'll make a note of it, Colonel," Captain Crawford said solemnly, writing something or other on his pad.

"Be particularly cautious now that we approach Christmas," I told Martin, who was baffled, utterly dismayed.

I went on to Woofer, looked him up and down critically, not favorably impressed, certainly. He was the only one of the three in uniform, but it was a worthless, tattered array, as sorry as I ever saw. He had no coat or jacket and was shivering. His toes stuck through the top of his shoes. "You been gambling with clothes as chips, soldier?" I asked him.

"Been giving away mostly, Owen," he said, papa's twisty grin sweeping over his face.

"What's your name?"

"James Pinkney Wright."

"Called Pink, are you?"

"Woofer."

"Why?"

"Because I woofed my food as a boy."

"Where you from?"

"Harristown, North Carolina."

"I know that place. There's no town there."

"I'll say there's not."

"Stand at attention, soldier," Captain Crawford commanded sharply.

"It's presumptuous of you to call it a town," I said to Woofer.

"All it has is a church and one mill. You wouldn't call it Harris City, would you?"

"And one smithy," Woofer said.

"Sir," Crawford corrected him. "One smithy, sir."

"You're not another one of that family of Wrights?" I said. "One of them came to the army a few years ago, a thief I'm told, for he stole from his father—"

"Not a thief, do you think, for he never got a cent," Woofer said.

"He threw the corn out of the crib and had the floor boards up, two bags of money in his hands—"

"He never got it away—"

"He was stealing, soldier—"

"Owen, you never got a cent of it, for papa and Jesse and Phillip come down on you—"

"Sir," Crawford reminded him. "Not Owen," he said.

"Not Owen? What you mean not Owen? It was Owen with the money in his hands the last night he was home."

"Sir! Say 'sir' when you address me too," Crawford said.

"Aw for law sake," Woofer said.

"I only know what's reported to me," I said. "This man Wright struck his father in the face with one of the bags, I hear, broke his chin."

"Why, you did not break his chin—"

"Then he started throwing money to the pigs—"

"Well, he never—you never stole, Owen."

"You are of that same family, that's the point of it?"

"Hell, yes," he said.

"When did you start cursing?"

"Everybody—Owen, it's the army."

"Sir," Crawford said.

"Sir," Woofer said.

"You're not a soldier yet," I said, "though if you're a Wright you're a born thief, a fugitive from your own home town, which is no town at all. Your brother is said to have climbed over the

21

bodies of other officers to get to be a colonel, a ruthlessly ambi-
tious man—as your two hutmates have already told you."

There was a sudden stiffening in the spines of the two hutmates. Betsy belched again. I knew I had struck home. All three
of them stared uneasily ahead now, all three stood solidly, rig-
idly at attention. I stepped back from them, looked them over
head to foot. "Put them on the list, Captain, for defaming an
officer."

"Yes, sir," Crawford said.

"Have them report at eight o'clock."

"Yes, sir," Crawford said.

"For two drinks of whiskey and two eggs apiece."

It was my habit at the close of inspection to release a few
animals for the men to catch—a greased pig and a greased
gander usually. I had to buy the animals with my own money,
having been forbidden by the army to use theirs for such a
practice, or even to continue it. This morning when the pig and
gander were released, the customary scramble began, the 300
soldiers converging to try to close off all escape, blocking and
striking one another, the men of a hut banding together to chase
the pig into their hut only to have the hut turned over and the
squealing pig let out. The goose was caught by Martin Luther
at one point; it flew into his scrawny arms. Martin was upturned
by the men, was right roughly treated—my men are not respect-
ers of anybody's person when a meal is in the offing, saint or
sinner. Much cursing. Much yelling. Many fist fights. Finally the
prizes were claimed and successfully defended. Much shouting,
celebrating.

As we walked to the headquarters building I asked Captain
Crawford how many men had been present and accounted for
at the inspection.

"Three hundred four," he said.

"That's all?"

"I'm not counting forty still in the hospitals, sir, including
Lieutenant King."

onfiscated. One night we began talking about why we had
1 the army. "I was out plowing for a woman north of
gh," I said, "and the train stopped and men got down and
a to water most everything and I said, 'Look, we plan to
potatoes there.' I recognized one man, then another; sev-
f them were from near home and I said what is it you're
, and they said there's a war, didn't you know that, and I
knew South Carolina and Virginia were at war, but are we
r too? Come on, they said, we'll win it in one fight, so I left
low and even left my coat because it was spring. I was
ing to be back, maybe by the next day. Then we got up
nassas, Virginia, and here came carriages from Richmond
ther places, people coming to see us beat the Yanks, and
; the little Bull Run River we could see the Yank army and
nad excursion trains and carriages that had been sent from
ington, full of congressmen and women, all waiting to see
anks beat the Rebels, neither side knowing quite what to
th their guns and flags. Oh my. My, my, it seems so long

1d we beat them," Betsy said.
ney won in the morning, and we won in the afternoon," I
'and they retreated in every direction. Well, it wasn't an
wasn't trained as such. We could have walked into Wash-
1, itself, if we had wanted anything the Yanks had, instead
t defending ourselves."
e should have," Betsy said.
oofer, why did you join?" I asked.
y woman," he said mournfully.
ughed out loud, surprised, it was such a bold claim for a
; man. "A woman?"
ofer groaned. "Will you help me with her, Owen?"
b, no," I said. "Not with any woman. I might take her for
f."
oined the army to get you to help me. I fear papa'll beat
1d me both when he finds out. And so will her people."

26

"How is he?"

"Recovering. It's expected he will be up and well soon."

"Three hundred and four? Report 350 to brigade headquarters."

He sighed. "This again breaks regulations, sir," he said sullenly.

"It might get the men extra food," I said.

"Also, I feel I should remind you again that general order 509
forbids goose or pig entertainments."

"Too dangerous for soldiers, are they?"

"Two of our men have broken their limbs on Sundays past."

"Yes, we must stop it, of course," I said, "come spring. Mark
it down, Captain."

And, so help me, he marked it down.

Why did I keep this persnickinish man always close by? I
can't very well answer, except to say, first, that he was accurate,
he did keep track of what was going on. It's a pleasure to know
when one is breaking an order, for instance, and to know its
number is the final touch of irony. Then, too, it pleased me to
have him here because back home he had been such a superior
little boy, always attended by a slave or two—even at church.
He always came to church in a carriage, not on foot, not in a
wagon even, mind you. He only lived a hundred yards away.
Rain or shine, that little boy came to church in a carriage. He
never came to school at all—it was held for six weeks most every
winter. He never came to play with us; his mother protected
him from us. He was some sort of special person. And when he
was twelve he was sent to East Tennessee to be educated, and
after that he went to a college for a year or two, later passed his
bar exam, developed the broad-A speech which Eastern planters have, most unlike the Western speech of our mountain section, which my family has, and Crawford's. One must dislike an
overly adaptable fellow of that sort. And when I got into this
regiment, there he was, a lieutenant, the rank given him because of his father's influence. Why, he was no soldier, believe

23

me. He froze with fright even when artillery was fired a mile away. I was a private soldier at that time, he was an officer, but I was made a lieutenant after my first battle, which I fought with General Jackson, and I went on in three months to be a captain, in ten months to be a major, finally to become a colonel, making swift advance, I must admit; two of my superiors were killed in battle, but two others were sent to the Western front. It's a common enough strategy. I think they suspected toward the close that I had been involved, and somehow the men also suspected me. They glean everything; within a few months they glean it all, true and false, and of course they believe it all, true and false, every rumor, including the current one that General Manger is ill and I will take over his brigade, of which my regiment is one of three.

Anyway, I became the regimental commander, and as the colonel I could advance one of my three lieutenants to captain or major, and I, who had been busy outmaneuvering superiors myself, advanced neither McGregor nor King, both excellent officers; I chose the Lieutenant to serve next to me who could never take my place, this fellow Crawford.

It soothed my soul to have him with me. He carried my pad and ink bottle around, and wrote reports for me, and wrote letters for me to sign, even attended boring administrative meetings on my behalf. I suppose I should have got a carriage and had him drive me to church on Sunday.

How cruel we are to our childhood friends—like children. How close and cruel children and men can be sometimes, as they seek the clasp of hand that is denied them.

On this particular Sunday we had our church service in the afternoon. The men were ordered to be present, but they did as they pleased. Here in December they were less interested in salvation than they would be later on, as battles became more likely. On this Sunday afternoon there were only 70 men present at the hillside where we met. The regimental chaplain had invited a visiting minister to preach. It was an honor at

home for a preacher to have preached to
suffered all too many of these different ones
old fellow I rather liked read his sermon fr
preaching to us on the subject of "Infant F
with a special appeal to mothers.

I always sat in the front row. It was und
my hat on, the preacher had in my opinio
and had best sit down. On this Sunday th
byterian, a Scot, and he resented my putt
he was only begun—he had spoken half a
off the platform, but he wouldn't go. Ster:
called me to preach, not you, Colonel W

"Yes, but I have called you to stop," I

"Colonel, I must complete the message
heart."

"Sergeant, take him to my place and l

"You will lock up a man of God?" he

"God has no trouble visiting you in jai
locked up most of the time."

"And if God damns your soul to hell

"Would he do that?"

"Aye. He would."

"Then he and I operate in much the
and waved the sergeant on.

The preacher, poor fellow, tried to ret:
pulled away, and he shouted out, "God

"I have no fear of hell, having seen the
which gave the men something to lau;
more to laugh about—except I noticed
Luther were not amused. They had inc
their faces and scowled at me woefully
be a disappointment to them again.

They and Betsy came by often of an
eggs and bacon and doused them wit

"How is he?"

"Recovering. It's expected he will be up and well soon."

"Three hundred and four? Report 350 to brigade headquarters."

He sighed. "This again breaks regulations, sir," he said sullenly.

"It might get the men extra food," I said.

"Also, I feel I should remind you again that general order 509 forbids goose or pig entertainments."

"Too dangerous for soldiers, are they?"

"Two of our men have broken their limbs on Sundays past."

"Yes, we must stop it, of course," I said, "come spring. Mark it down, Captain."

And, so help me, he marked it down.

Why did I keep this persnickinish man always close by? I can't very well answer, except to say, first, that he was accurate, he did keep track of what was going on. It's a pleasure to know when one is breaking an order, for instance, and to know its number is the final touch of irony. Then, too, it pleased me to have him here because back home he had been such a superior little boy, always attended by a slave or two—even at church. He always came to church in a carriage, not on foot, not in a wagon even, mind you. He only lived a hundred yards away. Rain or shine, that little boy came to church in a carriage. He never came to school at all—it was held for six weeks most every winter. He never came to play with us; his mother protected him from us. He was some sort of special person. And when he was twelve he was sent to East Tennessee to be educated, and after that he went to a college for a year or two, later passed his bar exam, developed the broad-A speech which Eastern planters have, most unlike the Western speech of our mountain section, which my family has, and Crawford's. One must dislike an overly adaptable fellow of that sort. And when I got into this regiment, there he was, a lieutenant, the rank given him because of his father's influence. Why, he was no soldier, believe me. He froze with fright even when artillery was fired a mile away. I was a private soldier at that time, he was an officer, but I was made a lieutenant after my first battle, which I fought with General Jackson, and I went on in three months to be a captain, in ten months to be a major, finally to become a colonel, making swift advance, I must admit; two of my superiors were killed in battle, but two others were sent to the Western front. It's a common enough strategy. I think they suspected toward the close that I had been involved, and somehow the men also suspected me. They glean everything; within a few months they glean it all, true and false, and of course they believe it all, true and false, every rumor, including the current one that General Manger is ill and I will take over his brigade, of which my regiment is one of three.

Anyway, I became the regimental commander, and as the colonel I could advance one of my three lieutenants to captain or major, and I, who had been busy outmaneuvering superiors myself, advanced neither McGregor nor King, both excellent officers; I chose the Lieutenant to serve next to me who could never take my place, this fellow Crawford.

It soothed my soul to have him with me. He carried my pad and ink bottle around, and wrote reports for me, and wrote letters for me to sign, even attended boring administrative meetings on my behalf. I suppose I should have got a carriage and had him drive me to church on Sunday.

How cruel we are to our childhood friends—like children. How close and cruel children and men can be sometimes, as they seek the clasp of hand that is denied them.

On this particular Sunday we had our church service in the afternoon. The men were ordered to be present, but they did as they pleased. Here in December they were less interested in salvation than they would be later on, as battles became more likely. On this Sunday afternoon there were only 70 men present at the hillside where we met. The regimental chaplain had invited a visiting minister to preach. It was an honor at home for a preacher to have preached to the troops, and we suffered all too many of these different ones to appear. One dear old fellow I rather liked read his sermon from yellowed paper, preaching to us on the subject of "Infant Baptism" and closing with a special appeal to mothers.

I always sat in the front row. It was understood that, if I put my hat on, the preacher had in my opinion exhausted his text and had best sit down. On this Sunday the visitor was a Presbyterian, a Scot, and he resented my putting my hat on when he was only begun—he had spoken half an hour. I waved him off the platform, but he wouldn't go. Sternly he told me, "God called me to preach, not you, Colonel Wright."

"Yes, but I have called you to stop," I said.

"Colonel, I must complete the message God has laid on my heart."

"Sergeant, take him to my place and let him finish it there."

"You will lock up a man of God?" he shouted.

"God has no trouble visiting you in jail," I said. "St. Paul was locked up most of the time."

"And if God damns your soul to hell for it—?"

"Would he do that?"

"Aye. He would."

"Then he and I operate in much the same manner," I said, and waved the sergeant on.

The preacher, poor fellow, tried to retain his dignity as he was pulled away, and he shouted out, "God will see you in hell, sir!"

"I have no fear of hell, having seen the Rebel army," I replied, which gave the men something to laugh about, or something more to laugh about—except I noticed that Woofer and Martin Luther were not amused. They had incredulous expressions on their faces and scowled at me woefully. I fear I had proved to be a disappointment to them again.

They and Betsy came by often of an evening, and I fed them eggs and bacon and doused them with whiskey and brandy I

25

had confiscated. One night we began talking about why we had joined the army. "I was out plowing for a woman north of Raleigh," I said, "and the train stopped and men got down and began to water most everything and I said, 'Look, we plan to plant potatoes there.' I recognized one man, then another; several of them were from near home and I said what is it you're doing, and they said there's a war, didn't you know that, and I said I knew South Carolina and Virginia were at war, but are we at war too? Come on, they said, we'll win it in one fight, so I left my plow and even left my coat because it was spring. I was planning to be back, maybe by the next day. Then we got up to Manassas, Virginia, and here came carriages from Richmond and other places, people coming to see us beat the Yanks, and across the little Bull Run River we could see the Yank army and they had excursion trains and carriages that had been sent from Washington, full of congressmen and women, all waiting to see the Yanks beat the Rebels, neither side knowing quite what to do with their guns and flags. Oh my. My, my, it seems so long ago."

"And we beat them," Betsy said.

"They won in the morning, and we won in the afternoon," I said, "and they retreated in every direction. Well, it wasn't an army, wasn't trained as such. We could have walked into Washington, itself, if we had wanted anything the Yanks had, instead of just defending ourselves."

"We should have," Betsy said.

"Woofer, why did you join?" I asked.

"My woman," he said mournfully.

I laughed out loud, surprised, it was such a bold claim for a young man. "A woman?"

Woofer groaned. "Will you help me with her, Owen?"

"No, no," I said. "Not with any woman. I might take her for myself."

"I joined the army to get you to help me. I fear papa'll beat her and me both when he finds out. And so will her people."

26